Annie's Plan

To George, for his constant love and support, and for those in Broward County who have chosen teaching as their profession — JK

To Tracy, my love and inspiration — CB

Published by
MAGINATION PRESS
An Educational Publishing Foundation Book
American Psychological Association
750 First Street, NE
Washington, DC 20002

For more information about our books, including a complete catalog, please write to us,
call 1-800-374-2721, or visit our website at www.maginationpress.com.

Editor: Darcie Conner Johnston
Art Director: Susan K. White
Printed by Worzalla, Stevens Point, Wisconsin

Library of Congress Cataloging-in-Publication Data

Kraus, Jeanne R.
Annie's plan : taking charge of schoolwork and homework / by Jeanne Kraus ;
illustrated by Charles Beyl.
p. cm.
Summary: With the help of her teacher and parents, Annie learns how to organize her desk,
pay attention in class, and prepare her homework assignments.
ISBN-13: 978-1-59147-481-4 (hardcover : alk. paper)
ISBN-10: 1-59147-481-7 (hardcover : alk. paper)
ISBN-13: 978-1-59147-482-1 (pbk. : alk. paper)
ISBN-10: 1-59147-482-5 (pbk. : alk. paper)
[1. Homework—Fiction. 2. Orderliness—Fiction. 3. Behavior—Fiction. 4. Schools—Fiction.]
I. Beyl, Charles, ill. II. Title.
PZ7.K8673Ann 2006
[Fic]—dc22
2006009948

10 9 8 7 6 5 4 3 2 1

Annie's Plan

Taking Charge of Schoolwork and Homework

written by Jeanne Kraus
illustrated by Charles Beyl

MAGINATION PRESS • WASHINGTON, D.C.

Annie was smart.
She *zoooomed* through chapter books.

She loved solving puzzles.

And sometimes she could add and subtract numbers even faster than her brother Christopher, who was in *fourth* grade.

At school
there was so
much to see...

...and so much to do.

While Mrs. Boyer described the pyramids of ancient Egypt,
Annie watched a bright red cardinal in the tree outside.
Did he have enough birdseed? Annie had a great idea!
She would make a bird feeder when she got home.

Mrs. Boyer talked about clouds, and the clouds reminded Annie
of a puff of dragon's breath. She drew a fire-breathing dragon
with beautiful scales, using her brand new colored pencils.

Annie admired her bracelet during journal time.

Off went the bracelet.

On went the bracelet.

What beautiful sparkles!

Off went the bracelet.

Oh no! Away went the bracelet!

Annie was surprised when kids got up to put their papers in the math basket. She had hardly started!

During literature time, the class read page 27 of *Skinny Cats*. But not Annie. She was still looking for her favorite pencil. She looked under her desk, in her desk, shook out her book... no pencil. Mrs. Boyer reminded Annie to open her book and focus on the poem.

"Tomorrow is a new day," Mrs. Boyer always reminded Annie.

A new day! Yes, tomorrow Annie would try harder. She would pay attention and listen. She would remember everything. She would finish all of her work. Mrs. Boyer would be proud. Mom and Dad would be proud too.

But there were days when Annie left her homework at school. And sometimes she just didn't remember what she was supposed to do. "I think it's page 31," she would say, or "Maybe I don't have math homework tonight."

It seemed like homework took forever.
Mom and Dad were annoyed a lot.

"You missed this page of subtraction facts," said Dad.
"You forgot to write a paragraph
about your favorite vacation," said Mom.
Why was this so hard? Annie was really trying!
And she knew that she was smart enough to do the work.

But the absolute worst thing was when Annie's homework wasn't in her backpack at school in the morning. And she was POSITIVE she had finished it!

"We need a plan," said Mrs. Boyer.

"We need a plan," said Mom and Dad.

"I need a plan," said Annie.

Annie's Plan
SCHOOLWORK

1. CLEAN DESK

2. SECRET REMINDERS TO FOCUS

3. STUDY BUDDY

4. DAILY GOALS

5. TEACHER TALKS AND SIGNALS

"Let's start with this desk," said Mrs. Boyer.
"We'll do this every Friday."

Annie stacked her schoolbooks on the shelf next to her desk.
It helped keep the inside of her desk more organized.

WOW! What a difference! No more hunting for buried treasure.

Mrs. Boyer gave Annie a "Do Now" red dot to stick on the corner of her desk. It was a secret reminder to pay attention to her work.

Mrs. Boyer asked Olivia to be Annie's study buddy. Olivia sat next to Annie and helped her when she had questions. Annie and Olivia exchanged phone numbers in case they had homework questions.

4. DAILY GOALS

Each morning, Annie and Mrs. Boyer decided on a daily goal.
It was hard for Annie to get going in the morning.
A slow start could ruin her day.
So her first goal was *Begin morning work promptly.*
Mrs. Boyer made a weekly reminder card for Annie to tape to her desk.
The first week it read:

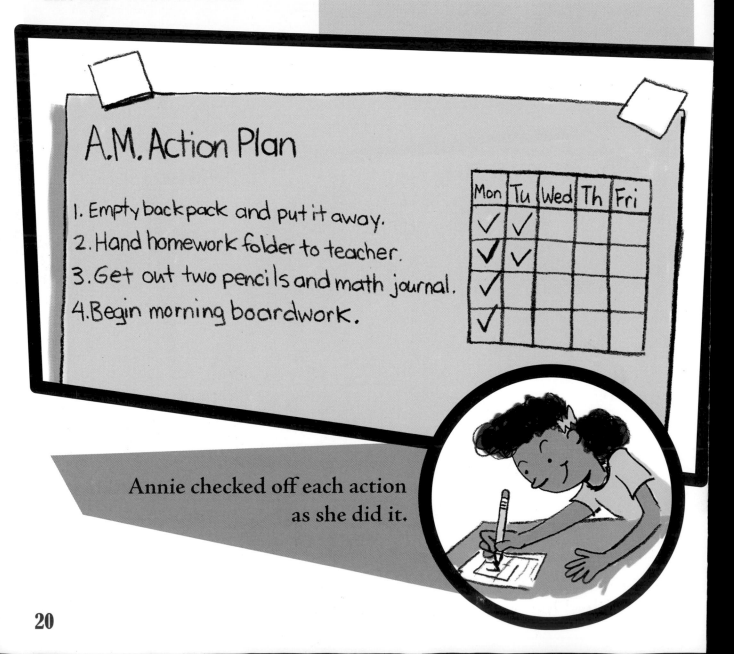

A.M. Action Plan

1. Empty backpack and put it away.
2. Hand homework folder to teacher.
3. Get out two pencils and math journal.
4. Begin morning boardwork.

	Mon	Tu	Wed	Th	Fri
	✓	✓			
	✓	✓			
	✓				
	✓				

Annie checked off each action as she did it.

Throughout the day, Mrs. Boyer winked at Annie,
their secret signal that Annie was doing well with her daily goals.

5. TEACHER TALKS AND SIGNALS

Mrs. Boyer had quiet little talks with just Annie.
She encouraged her and said nice things about her work.

THINK TANK

6. QUIET WORK AREA

Annie could choose to work in the Think Tank,
the quiet area where kids went when they needed to concentrate.
Annie liked having a choice of where to work.

7. DAILY PLANNER

Every afternoon Annie wrote her homework assignments in her daily planner. Mrs. Boyer made sure Annie remembered everything. Then she signed it.

MARCH

SUNDAY 26

MONDAY 27 Mrs. B.
Write Sp. words 3x each
Read 20 Minutes

TUESDAY 28 Mrs. B.
Pratice Math flash cards
Read 20 Minutes
Spelling Words — ABC order

WEDNESDAY 29 Mrs. B.
Use 6 Sp. Words in a story
Read 20 Minutes

THURSDAY 30 Mrs. B.
Math Riddles
Study for Sp. Test
Practice lines for Play!

FRIDAY 31 Mrs. B.
Read a book to someone
Write a paragraph about the main character

SATURDAY 1
Gory Stories!

MONDAY
Annie needs pencils and notebook paper -- Mrs Boyer
☑ SCHOOL ☐ HOME

We're helping Annie create her own study area! - Annie's Mom
☐ SCHOOL ☒ HOME

Annie is remembering to raise her hand - Good job!
☑ SCHOOL ☐ HOME - Mrs Boyer

Annie can't find her library book - Mrs Boyer
☑ SCHOOL ☐ HOME

SHE FOUND IT! - ANNIE'S DAD
☐ SCHOOL ☒ HOME

Spelling Words

train

sale

place

gray

22

Annie took her assignments home in a blue homework folder.

Each morning Annie handed the whole folder to her teacher when they talked about her daily goal.

Annie met with the guidance counselor.
Mrs. Parks invited her to join the Study Skills Club.
They ate lunch together every Monday
and talked about homework tips and how to study for tests.

Annie also knew she could visit the counselor
any time she felt worried or frustrated or upset.

10. REWARD CONTRACT

Mrs. Parks helped Annie and her teacher make a contract. Mrs. Boyer gave Annie smiley faces for finishing her work and meeting her daily goals. When Annie earned enough smiley faces, she could be a buddy reader in kindergarten or be Mrs. Boyer's teaching assistant.

She REALLY liked being a teaching assistant!

Annie's Plan
HOMEWORK

Annie cleaned out her backpack. Only school stuff stayed in.
Pencils went in a pencil case. Fresh notebook paper had its own
folder. A book for independent reading went in a zipper compartment.

Her parents helped her by checking her backpack
every night after Homework Time.

2. SPECIAL HOMEWORK AREA

Annie's homework was her job, just like being a teacher was Mrs. Boyer's job. She would need her own special place in order to do her best work. Annie put up a sign.

Do Not Disturb
Student at Work

Everything had its place—pencils, erasers, markers, paper, dictionary. No supply searches during Homework Time!

3. SCHEDULED HOMEWORK TIME

"My work hours are 5:30 to 6:30,
Monday through Thursday," Annie announced.
"That's after something fun, and before dinner."

4. NO INTERRUPTIONS

No telephone or TV
during Homework Time.
Annie told her friends she was not available then.

5. PRIORITIZE ASSIGNMENT ORDER

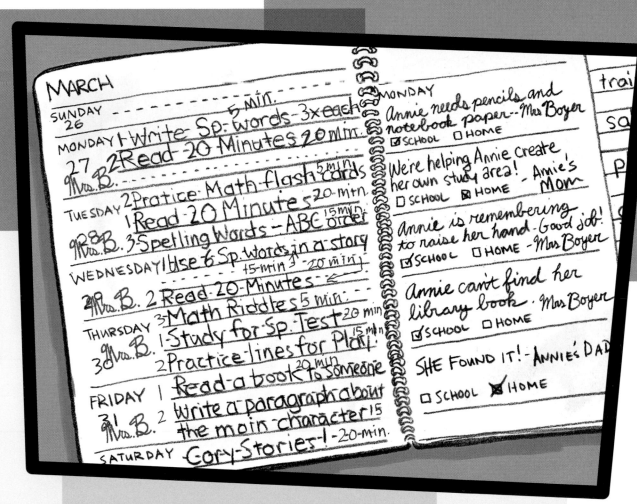

Annie and her parents checked her planner to decide what to do first. They called it prioritizing assignments. She decided to save her favorite subject for last.

6. ESTIMATE ASSIGNMENT TIME

Annie also estimated how much time each assignment would take.

7. HOME WORK BREAKS

Annie set the timer for her first assignment.
"No mind breaks until then," she said.

When the timer dinged, she set it for 5 minutes.
Then she stretched and did ten jumping jacks.

After her break, she was ready for Assignment Number 2.
"Subtraction facts will take 15 minutes."

8. PARENT CHECKS

When she finished all of her assignments, her parents checked her work. "Wow, looks like you did it all!" They signed her planner.

9. PREPARE FOR TOMORROW

Annie put all of her homework in the blue homework folder.

She put the homework folder and her planner in her backpack.

She sharpened her pencils and put them in the pencil case in her backpack.

She checked the notebook paper folder in her backpack.

She cleaned up her study area. "Ready for tomorrow," she said.

She put the backpack by the front door in her new Go-to-School Bin.

"What's for dinner?" she asked.

10. REWARDS

Mom and Dad gave Annie a big hug.
They also gave her a star sticker to put on her calendar.
"Ten stars will equal a reward!"

The next day, when Annie handed in her homework folder, Mrs. Boyer gave her their secret wink...and a smiley face.

And at 3:15 Mrs. Boyer didn't say, "Tomorrow is a new day." She said, "Great day, Annie!"

Annie's Plan was working. Now *every* day could be a great day!

Note to Parents and Educators

Good habits don't always come naturally. For children who have problems with organization and attention, learning study skills and work habits may be an especially tough challenge.

Parents, teachers, and other education staff can help by implementing systems for staying organized and by encouraging feelings of responsibility, control, and empowerment. The ten tips outlined in each of Annie's plans—one for schoolwork and one for homework—are simple yet effective strategies for acquiring the skills and habits that are a foundation for academic success.

With Annie's Plan, every day can be a great day!

Annie's Plan:
S C H O O L W O R K

An uncluttered desk is crucial to keeping track of papers, books, and supplies. Teachers can stress the value of a neat desk, and help children maintain one in the following ways:

Weekly desk inspections and "clean desk" certificates are great incentives for staying on top of clutter. If children sit in groups, then points can be given to groups for keeping their area clean. Here is where peer pressure can aid the teacher in achieving progress toward classroom organization.

Help children create good, simple systems for keeping materials organized. For example, color-coded subject folders help organize papers inside the desk. Pencils and erasers should be kept in a zippered pouch or box with a snap lid.

If the child is sitting near a bookcase, shelf, or empty desk, allow the child to put textbooks there, with spines out for easy identification, so that more space is available for organization inside the desk.

A visual reminder may assist children in staying focused without singling them out in front of the class. The signal can be a sticker, card, or dot attached to the desk to remind them, for example, to begin their morning warm-up as soon as they enter the classroom and unpack.

A reminder of classroom procedures can also be posted prominently for all children to see.

Inattentive children do best when seated near the teacher during instruction time, with their chair facing the area in which the teacher is demonstrating the lesson. Walking by these children during instruction, putting your hand on their shoulder, and pointing to their work as you go by all help to keep the child focused.

Children who are disorganized or inattentive often benefit from a peer's guidance and help. This is especially important for homework help and during guided reading groups, when the teacher is not always available to answer questions.

Many peer tutors are excellent role models and enjoy helping others. Make sure that the student is comfortable about accepting help from a peer and that the study buddy is motivated to be of help without being impatient or negative.

Conference with the buddy periodically to make sure the partnership is productive and the buddy is not showing signs of stress. Remember that buddies need positive reinforcement too!

For children who have trouble focusing, getting started, and staying on task, an A.M. Action Plan shows the child's

responsibilities when entering the classroom each day. This plan can be written on an index card and taped to the child's desk. For younger children, use pictures as visual cues of what to do first, second, and so forth. This type of structure starts each day on a positive note.

A typical A.M. Action list might include:
- Enter the room quietly.
- Empty backpack and put away.
- Put away lunch.
- Hand in homework.
- Take out math journal and sharpened pencils.
- Begin math problems on the board.

Setting daily short-term goals with the teacher can further help children structure themselves. In choosing goals, the parents, teacher, and child should together discuss areas of weakness that can be addressed. Parents can reinforce the goal at home in the morning with gentle reminders and encouragement. When the child arrives at school, the teacher quickly reviews the goal with him or her immediately upon arrival: "Today your goal is to see if you can follow the morning action plan on your own. I know you can do it!"

A little feedback from the teacher can go a long way in motivating a child in the right direction. Once the teacher and child have talked briefly about the daily goal, the teacher can help shape behavior by noticing the child working toward the goal. A secret signal, such as a wink or "thumbs up," assures children that their efforts are being noticed and that they are progressing well.

Teachers show respect for their students' self-esteem and dignity by communicating with them privately about their progress. They can easily take advantage of quiet moments on the way to lunch, at recess, or before dismissal to share a quick word of positive feedback or guidance with children.

Frequent pep talks help motivate children and encourage them to focus on their goals. Positive comments and praise should be specific and target the desired behavior. For example, "Good work!" doesn't specify what you are praising, but a comment such as "You did a great job remembering to turn in your homework this morning" is more meaningful and empowering.

Some children have difficulty sitting near other children. But if they are isolated from the rest of the class for long periods of time, they do not learn to limit their off-task behavior. Children need to learn to be able to monitor their distractions.

A positive alternative is to have a Think Tank area in the classroom where children can go any time they need a quiet place to work. This can be a table or a group of desks that are situated away from areas where conversation may occur frequently.

Make it a class rule that children are allowed to use the Think Tank when they need to concentrate.

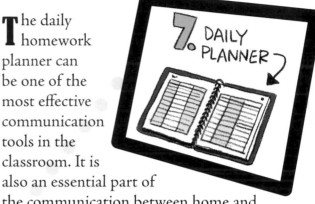

The daily homework planner can be one of the most effective communication tools in the classroom. It is also an essential part of the communication between home and school. Many schools provide a planner for each student in grades 1 through 5.

The success of the planner depends on consistent use. Ideally, time is set aside for organizing homework before dismissal every school day. At this time, the teacher explains or demonstrates how to write the homework as students copy it down in their planner. This process helps to alleviate homework problems:

- Create a visual display of how the homework planner should look. The pages of the planner can be shown to the class on an overhead projector, for example.
- Go over each assignment separately, having the children highlight the directions and key words. Do an example together.
- If spelling words are to be written in the planner, a correct list of the words could be placed (preferably stapled) inside the planner. If children copy the words incorrectly, they will study incorrect spelling all week!

Teachers schedule planner checks every morning, usually as the children complete their daily morning assignment. Missing or incomplete assignments can be noted in the planner.

Consistent use of the planner is vital not only for the children but also for their parents, who depend on it as a communication tool at home. Many teachers write notes to parents in the planner and encourage parents to respond. Parents' concerns are addressed during the morning check, and teachers can monitor that parents have signed the planner. Thanks to the planner, all members of the team are on the same page!

Many schools have a special pocket folder that goes home with each child every day.

One side of the folder may be designated Things That Stay Home, for notices and graded papers for parents to view. The other side of the folder may be designated Things That Need to Come Back to School. Notices that need to be signed and returned, homework, and so forth are placed in this side. Teachers usually go over the homework system with parents during a school's Open House or Back-to-School Night.

Having a planned place and system for carrying homework and other school papers is a great organizational tool. As the child develops the habit of making sure the folder is in the backpack at the beginning and end of the day, the problem of forgetting or losing items will decrease.

It is always helpful for children to realize that other students have some of the same organizational difficulties that they have. A small academic support group can have very positive effects on confidence and self-esteem.

Study clubs can be organized by the guidance counselor or curriculum specialist, and facilitated by teachers, paraprofessionals, or trained volunteers. A typical group might have five or six students and meet for an hour two days a week for homework planning, prioritizing assignments, and learning how to manage time effectively. Part of the time is spent on working on homework with the assistance of the trained adult. At the end of the meeting, children are asked to think about such questions as:

🖉 What worked for you today?
🖉 How did you help yourself?
🖉 What do you want to do differently tomorrow?

Peer tutoring clubs can also be very effective at schools that provide after-school care for students. One of the selected activities could be a homework session with adult counselors or upper-grade tutors. A little help goes a long way!

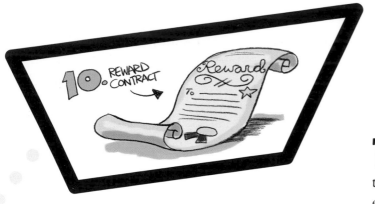

Annie's Plan:
HOMEWORK

The school guidance counselor is a great resource for helping support students' individual needs. A teacher may meet with the counselor to discuss a student and draw up a reward contract tailored for him or her.

The contract keeps track of daily accomplishments, and may address such desired skills as "brings in homework," "uses time wisely," or "has all needed supplies." Each day the student earns a mark (e.g., star, sticker, or smiley face) for each skill completed successfully, and at the end of the week he or she receives a reward based on the number of marks earned.

Rewards may include lunch with a special adult, stickers, pencils, and certificates. As children progress, they may earn the privilege to be a helper in the art room, library, cafeteria, and so on. Most students love to be helpers, but those who have difficulty finishing their work on time are usually not called upon for classroom assistance. Allowing these children to help others as they become more responsible is very positive reinforcement.

The backpack is the vehicle that transports everything from school to home and back again. A well-organized backpack helps children keep track of homework, books, supplies, and communications between school and home. Running out of supplies, losing homework, and forgetting important items such as the daily planner are problems that diminish when the backpack is neat.

Make cleaning out the backpack a regular weekly routine. Pick a day and a time, and stick with it so that it becomes a habit. (Parents might clean out a briefcase or purse at the same time!) Here are a few pointers:

The first time or two, parents can demonstrate how to organize a backpack. Show that there is a place for everything. Then have your child do the organizing as you observe.

Have a list of basic school supplies posted at home, and check it every week during backpack clean-up. Be sure to keep supplies on hand to refill any that are depleted.

"A place for everything, and everything in its place" should be your child's motto. Loose papers always go in folders. Small items like pencils need to be in a case or pouch.

Even if the school doesn't supply one, keep a homework folder in the backpack. In earlier grades, one folder for all assignments works well. Older children may use colored folders for different subject areas, or a binder with color-coded subject areas. Homework should never be folded into the pages of the textbook.

Backpacks are for school materials only. Games and personal items clutter the backpack and distract the child, and should be left at home. Food and drinks, when needed, should be carried in a separate bag or lunchbox.

A designated area for homework facilitates the homework habit. This may be a desk area in the bedroom if the child works well without monitoring. If a child needs to work with more supervision, though, the kitchen or dining room table may be the best place. The kitchen or dining room also works well for children who want a parent nearby; they are more comfortable, and you can encourage their independence by easing yourself away as they are working. The important thing is that it's the same place every day, all supplies are at hand, and distractions are minimal.

Help your child fill a box with needed study supplies so that there is no search break during study time. Such supplies include a pencil sharpener and pencils, eraser, ruler, compass, glue stick, timer, notebook paper, sticky notes, markers, highlighters, tape, scissors, stapler, and bookmark.

Keep a dictionary in the study area, as well as any other reference books the child might be using.

Make the study area special with a Do Not Disturb sign.

Avoid distractions in the study area. For example, the TV should be off, younger children should be playing elsewhere, and telephone calls and other conversations within the child's earshot should be kept to a minimum. However, some children work better with soft classical or instrumental music playing in the background than with total silence. Experiment to find how your child works best.

M ake homework time a priority by scheduling it regularly, just as you would soccer practice and music lessons. Settle on the same time each day, and allow an appropriate amount of time, depending on the child's grade in school and the typical homework load. Check with the teacher to find out how much time the child is expected to spend on homework on a typical day.

In deciding on the best time for homework, take into account how your child performs right after school, after a little fun time, or after dinner. One child's productive period can be quite different from another's.

Show your child how important the homework period is by not scheduling conflicting activities for the child or the family. If you make it a priority, so will your child. You may want or need to modify a child's schedule if he or she takes on activities that are of value, such as a seasonal sport. Such changes should only be to accommodate significant activities, though, and you'll want to make sure that homework continues to be viewed as the top priority.

On days when your child says, "No homework, I finished it at school," maintain the scheduled time in order to keep the momentum going. Some children rush through their work before they come home so they can play. Let them know that if they already did their homework, there will be an independent reading time or perhaps time to study math facts.

If you find that homework is taking longer than it should or longer than the teacher expects, notify the teacher. Together you should be able to figure out what the problem is and find ways to resolve it.

Part of respecting the importance of homework time is ensuring that interruptions are kept to a minimum. Children can let their friends know in advance that they are unavailable during this period. Agree together that the child won't answer the phone or the doorbell until the period is over.

If there are small children in the house, this may be a good time for a nap or a quiet board game away from the homework area. Perhaps a teenager needs service hours for high school and may be called in to help. Be creative!

Last, bathroom breaks and snacks or drinks should be taken care of before the child begins to work.

Part of homework planning is deciding the order in which to do assignments. Help your child learn to prioritize by asking these questions:

- What do I have to do tonight?
- What is not due until next week?
- Which is the hardest assignment?
- Which is my favorite one?
- Which will take the longest?

The answers to these questions will help your child decide what to do first, second, and so forth. All work is most likely to get completed accurately if harder subjects come first and favorite subjects come last. Each child is different, though. Some may be more motivated if they put a longer assignment behind them right away, while others may want to do a shorter one to gain an early sense of accomplishment. Observe your child over time to see how he or she best stays on-task.

Working with the assignment list in the daily planner, demonstrate how to number assignments in the order they'll be done. Write the order in the planner. Any assignment that is not due immediately should be written down in the planner each day until the date it is due.

Continue to help your child prioritize assignments as long as needed by asking him or her to verbalize the questions out loud and to number the assignments in order.

Around third grade, children can continue to develop their independent work habits by estimating how long each assignment will take. Have children estimate how long they think each assignment will take, and write the estimate in the planner. By penciling in an estimate next to each assignment, children are learning to set goals to manage their time. These mini-goals aid in independent self-monitoring behavior.

On a practical level, estimating time helps students decide how to prioritize their daily assignments. It is also a good tool for planning a project that will be completed over a longer period of time, such as a report or a science fair entry.

Children love to use timers. Have them set a timer to see how far they get in their estimated time. Remind them often that it will take practice before their estimates are close.

Challenge your child to see if he or she can complete an assignment *carefully* within a designated time. Emphasize that speed is not the desired behavior. Instead, the goals are on-task behavior and the growing ability to plan.

It's unrealistic to expect children to remain focused on homework for long stretches of time. Without breaks, an elementary school-age child is likely to grow restless or careless, start to daydream, and look for distractions. Breaks should be a planned part of homework time, especially if homework time is longer than 30 minutes. In addition to keeping the child on-task, planned breaks give kids an empowering sense of control.

As children prioritize their assignments and number them in the planner, they can plan when to take a brief stretching break. Again, each child is different, and parents will need to assist with the planning of breaks. Trial and error will determine how long the child can stay focused before taking a break. Younger or more active children may need to stretch after each subject. By grade 2 most children can work 15-20 minutes.

Break time should be just a minute or two. Toe touches and finger exercises are great ways to refocus energy and prepare for the next assignment.

At the end of homework time, review your child's work. Your child needs to know that you value all homework efforts. Look for quality: Does it have a proper heading? Were directions followed? Is all of the homework completed? Is it readable? Are sentences complete? Are words spelled correctly?

Homework should be in the same place every night and ready for you to review. Quality tends to decline if parents are not involved in checking the work nightly, so be sure to make it a routine part of your evening. This nightly review also alerts you to any problems your child may be having in school.

Parents may sign the planner, noting they have seen the homework. Stay in contact with the teacher via the planner regarding any complications. Teachers appreciate parents' involvement, and contact can clear up any misunderstandings that your child may have passed along to you about the homework.

What about those frantic mornings when children can't find their homework, backpacks, or books? This is not the way to start off a day—for children or their parents!

Help your child get organized for the next day as soon as homework is finished and you've reviewed it. A checklist for children to follow is an ideal way to help while giving the responsibility to them. Post the checklist in the homework area. Items on the list might include:

- Homework in homework folder.
- Homework folder in backpack.
- Planner in backpack.
- Books in backpack.

- Pencil case in backpack.
- Check notebook paper supply.
- Library tomorrow? Need books.
- Gym tomorrow? Need shoes.

Keep a special bin or box by the front door for the backpack and other school items needed the next day. The beginning of the school day should be relaxed and happy.

A reward system at home can be a final tool to empower school-age children to develop the homework habit, get organized, and take on responsibility. It can be as simple as a star for each day that all items are checked off on a list that might include:

- Begin homework on time.
- Complete all homework in planner.
- Clean up study area.
- Put backpack by front door.

The list could also include related items, such as:

- Be ready for school on time.
- Read for 20 minutes.

The list can be more inclusive as the child gets older.

A star is earned for each successful day, and when a certain number are earned (e.g., 7 to 10), the child earns a reward. The best rewards are gifts of time and special attention, such as a favorite dinner, a game with Dad, the next book in a favorite series, or a sleepover with a friend. Avoid the trip to the toy store. Talk to your child about what he or she finds most meaningful, and come up with a list of rewards together.

The Importance of Practice

The value of schoolwork and homework is in the process as well as the product, fostering good habits of responsibility, organization, and self-motivation. Completing schoolwork and homework helps children develop skills that they need to become independent, motivated adults. And developing these good habits takes practice.

Reassure your children that these habits and skills develop over time, with practice, and not immediately. With each year, their ability to "own" their work will increase. This is the goal.

Collaboration is key. When teachers and families work together, students get the biggest benefit. Parents and teachers who communicate actively and who commit to strong organizational plans for their children encourage the skills that children need to be motivated learners. And when parents and teachers are dedicated to the development of independent work habits, they are also encouraging a love of learning that will last a lifetime.

About the Author

JEANNE KRAUS is a teacher and an educational specialist with expertise in attention disorders. A frequent speaker at conferences and workshops, she presents on such topics as organizational and study skills, parenting, and classroom management tips and instructional strategies for teachers. She lives in Broward County, Florida, and is the mother of two sons, one of whom inspired her first book, *Cory Stories: A Kid's Book About Living with ADHD*.

About the Illustrator

CHARLES BEYL creates humorous illustrations for books, magazines, and newspapers from his studio high atop an old Pennsylvania farmhouse. He is surrounded there by his family and his personal assistant, Iris, a six-year-old black Labrador. Look for more of his work in *My Parents Are Divorced Too*, *Learning to Slow Down and Pay Attention*, and *Blue Cheese and Stinky Feet: How to Deal with Bullies*.